THE SKY COLORED SHORE (AN INTRODUCTION)

THE EYES VENTURE INTO IMMENSE POSSIBILITIES OF FINDING HAPPINESS

ROHIT

Made with ❤ on the Notion Press Platform
www.notionpress.com

For Anna and Robben!!!! Enlightening the Future................

Contents

Foreword

The human endeavours are full of optimism and always venture into experimenting positively inclined joyful and ambitious things.

Preface

Very little has been achieved in exploring human joy and existence. An experiment into opening the pandora box of hope, happiness and wisdom. The book is a creative aspect which trails to adventures yet to be understood, explored and adopted.

CHAPTER ONE

THE ARRIVAL

Katherine reached Paris after a missed flight episode in the summer of 2018 after a long journey from Sydney enroute muscat. On arrival, the sight of the blue sky was mesmerizing that day as was eminent from the corridor on de-boarding the Oman Air Flight. The orange scarf flew with the breeze as and when the automatic glass door opened and closed with passengers crossing to and fro. Just then with a strong gust of wind the orange scarf fluttered and flew away from Katherines' shoulder and off it went rolling and swindling into the corridors of Paris airport. Playfully yet carefully, Katherine chased the scarf and with few missed chances of catching it finally succeeded in enrolling the beautiful orange scarf in her hands.

Her father and mother were happy and joyful to have arrived at the fashion capital of the world and had so much to achieve and do with things scribbled in the checklist and other things in their minds. They all looked into each others' eyes and hoped in anticipation to achieve their ambition. The sparkle in the eyes, the smile on the faces and curiosity in the minds, marks the beginning of the aspirations. Katherine had long curly brown hair and flawless skin with a bluish tint in her wide open eyes. The natural fragrance around Katherine caught everyone's attention and induced a sort of magical happiness in the proximity. The giggle and the glares are the most astonishing visual sightings that induces the good vibes in and around the people.

CHAPTER TWO

THE GESTURE

Katherine and her parents boarded a Mercedes cab and reached Anna's house to retire for the evening and spend their much awaited holiday. The ride was racy and culminated to hair raising experience through the streets of France. Anna welcomed them with heart wide open and showed the lavish villa with the kitchenette and various accessories. Katherine was curious to see the whole set of accessories and the garden and the flowers and the swimming pool at one go.

Anna offered some chocolates and coffee. She was concerned about the guests and never wanted to leave them alone. She had plans to serve then fresh juice with baked croissants. Katherine gifted the scarf to Anna as a gesture of love and compassion for all the care Anna showered on all three of them. Anna wore the sacred beads on her wrists with various religious inscriptions on the beads. Seeing the inquisitiveness around, she responded to the silence and said that Robben takes her to various mediational avenues to bring in spiritualism. Anna's voice was not only soft but had lot of emotions embedded in each string of word she spelt. She fell in love with the beautiful eyes of Katherine and could not take her eyes off Katherine. She admired the conduct and elegance of Katherine and her family. She handed over the keys of the Villa to them and bid them goodbye for the day. Never wanting to leave them alone she left so that they can take adequate rest. After rounds of shower, they awaited the sunset. The sky turned red with the glares of the setting sun and was shining on the faces of Katherine and her parents.

CHAPTER THREE

THE ROSE

They didn't realise the jet lag made their sleep cycle set early and the sun rays of the rising sun woke them up. Ronny was the first one to wake up and glanced through the window to ambitiously look towards the opportunities lying ahead. Alice was fully cheered up to be in Paris and passionately prepared tea and lifted Katherine into her arms in joy. Alice kissed Katherine and hugged Ronny in joy and happiness. They got ready for the day and started of the day on foot and reached a flower shop. The flowers smelled awesome and created a sparkle in their eyes. Ronny picked up pace and started walking speedily in his search for the unknown. They sat on a cafes' bench to have tasted the flavour of Rose Vine. The shopping followed and the mesmerising sight of architecture buildings made their day. Rose was a rose coloured commonly available vine. French people were relishing Rose in Goblets in cafes facing the sunset. Ronny and Alice filled the glasses with a fresh Rose and cheered and looked into eyes of Katherine and showed contentment in reaching the city of famous architects. Ronny had a passion to embrace the new things coming in the journey called life. He used to spend hours together imagining the underlying principles of the curious facts.

The Rose experiment was one of them. With bright sunrays striking the forehead, Ronny endured the experimental thinking and with a scent of rose felt the taste leading to the unthinkable possibilities of mixing different proportions of various flavours of grapes and quenching thirst of the travellers. The drowsiness was one of the grey areas to work upon when sitting under the sun and trying the Rose.

CHAPTER FOUR

SHADOW ON THE SEINE

As they embarked onto this beautiful journey, little they knew how the sky will change their lives and fortunes forever. Ronny had lot of hopes running in his mind and was constantly in search of the unknown. Alice was always embracing Katherine to be with her in each of the mesmerizing moments. The dry wood cranked and the footprints marked the old wooden bridge over the Seine. The searcher Ronny lay his eyes on the million locks locked on the rusty lamp post over the bridge and sighed in hope again. The sky was blue with snowy clouds sparkling the light into the eyes of the travel frontiers. Alice found a small pathway leading to one of the shores of Seine and nothing could stop Katherine from following her mothers' shadow. Ronny on the other hand followed them at ease as he knew the blue sky gods are protecting them as they were on a journey to find joy. As they walked arms in arms the musical rhythm started growing louder and louder as they approached the splashing sound of the flowing water. They increased their pace and started walking and drifting and running towards the music. The flute, the singing and the dance tapping were in the sighting on a small cruise boat with people holding champaignes and the vine glasses dancing and cheering in happiness. As the cruise moved and passed their sight the started walking matching pace with the cruise. The shining sun had drained out lot of sweat through the day and the sun rays were not slanting as the ticks of the clock progressed into the evening.

Ronny touched the cool water of Seine and splashed it onto Katherine and Alice. In a playful mood, Katherine clapped into the shore splashing the water joyfully. Alice held Katherine warmly in her arms and their she showed the magical shadow on the Seine. Katherine was experiencing the shadow and its understanding for the first time in her life. As she laughed, the shadow on seine laughed. As she clapped, the shadow on the seine followed and the expressions, cheer and gestures. It gave back all in the same form and led to further trials of human curiosity. Ronny now had a firm belief that the human endeavours are full of optimism and always venture into experimenting positively inclined joyful and ambitious things.